Look for these Just Right Books™

Just Right for 2's and 3's

HOW MANY KISSES GOOD NIGHT
By Jean Monrad/Illustrated by Eloise Wilkin

MINE! A SESAME STREET BOOK ABOUT SHARING
By Linda Hayward/Illustrated by Norman Gorbaty

THE NOISY COUNTING BOOK
By Susan Schade and Jon Buller

THE RAINY DAY PUDDLE
By Ei Nakabayashi

SALLY WANTS TO HELP
By Cindy Wheeler

SOUNDS MY FEET MAKE
By Arlene Blanchard/Illustrated by Vanessa Julian-Ottie

Just Right for 3's and 4's

THE JUST RIGHT MOTHER GOOSE
By Arnold Lobel

THE RUNAWAY CHRISTMAS TOY
By Linda Hayward/Illustrated by Ann Schweninger

SWEETIE AND PETIE
By Katharine Ross/Illustrated by Lisa McCue

UNDER THE MOON
By Joanne Ryder/Illustrated by Cheryl Harness

Just Right for 4's and 5's

THE CLEVER CARPENTER
By R. W. Alley

DOLLHOUSE MOUSE
By Natalie Standiford/Illustrated by Denise Fleming

PATRICK AND TED RIDE THE TRAIN
By Geoffrey Hayes

TIDY PIG
By Lucinda McQueen and Jeremy Guitar

Library of Congress Cataloging-in-Publication Data:
Ryder, Joanne. Under the moon / by Joanne Ryder ; illustrated by Cheryl Harness.   p.   cm.—(A Just right book) SUMMARY: Mama Mouse teaches her little mouse how to tell where home is by reminding her of its special smells, sounds, and textures.   ISBN: 0-394-81960-8 (trade); 0-394-91960-2 (lib. bdg.)   [1. Mice—Fiction.] I. Harness, Cheryl, ill. II. Title. III. Series: Just right books (New York, N.Y.) PZ7.R959Un 1989 [E] 88-11512

Manufactured in the United States of America   1 2 3 4 5 6 7 8 9 0

JUST RIGHT BOOKS is a trademark of Random House, Inc.

A Just Right Book

Under the Moon

By Joanne Ryder
Illustrated by Cheryl Harness

Random House 🏠 New York

One bright, clear evening Mama Mouse led her youngest mouse from place to place to teach her special things.

She showed her where to find the fattest seeds and the sweetest berries to eat.

She showed her tiny places under logs and snug spots inside bushes where she could hide when the owl flew by.

And then Mama said to her little mouse, "Let's go home now. Do you know where home is, little one?"

"Oh, yes, I know," said the little mouse. "We live under the moon."

"Under the moon!" said her mama. "Why, yes, I guess we do. But a little mouse needs to know more than that.

"Tell me, little one, can you remember what it smells like in our home under the moon?"

"I remember tingly smells," said the little mouse, "like the smell of warm blackberries in the sun and the smell of cool grass after the rain."

"Does it smell like that here?" asked Mama.

"No," said the little mouse, wiggling her nose and sniffing the leaves and moss and the brown roots that curled in and out of the ground. "It smells old and damp."

"You're right," said Mama. "This is the woods, and we don't live here."

"Can you tell me, little one," said Mama, "what it sounds like at home?"

"I remember singing," said the little mouse. "Tiny crickets chirp and chirp all night long at home."

"What else?" asked her mama.

"The wind," said the very small mouse. "I remember the wind whispering through the grass."

"Do you hear those things here?" asked her mama.

"No," said the little mouse. "I hear water bubbling over rocks and someone fast splashing in the water."

"Very good," said her mama. "This is the stream, and we don't live here."

"Can you tell me what it feels like when you're home?" asked Mama Mouse.

"It is warm at home," said the little mouse, "warm and soft. There are small, furry mice all around me. They tickle me with their whiskers, and they touch me with their soft paws.

"I know I live in a soft place under the moon."

"Is it soft here?" asked her mama.

"No," said the little mouse. "It is hard and rough here. Sharp pebbles slip under my feet, and it is empty all around."

Just then the little mouse heard a roar, and she and her mama leaped from the rocky place into a bush as something loud rushed past.

"This is a road," said her mama. "No animals live here. Remember, little one! This is not a safe place for you."

"It is getting late," said Mama, and she led the tiny mouse up and up, over a hilly place. They ran from bush to bush, stopping to rest under the biggest one.

The little mouse peeked between the branches and saw the stars twinkling far away. When the wind came and tickled the leaves, she saw the bright moon shining high above her.

"Look, Mama," she whispered. "It's our moon."

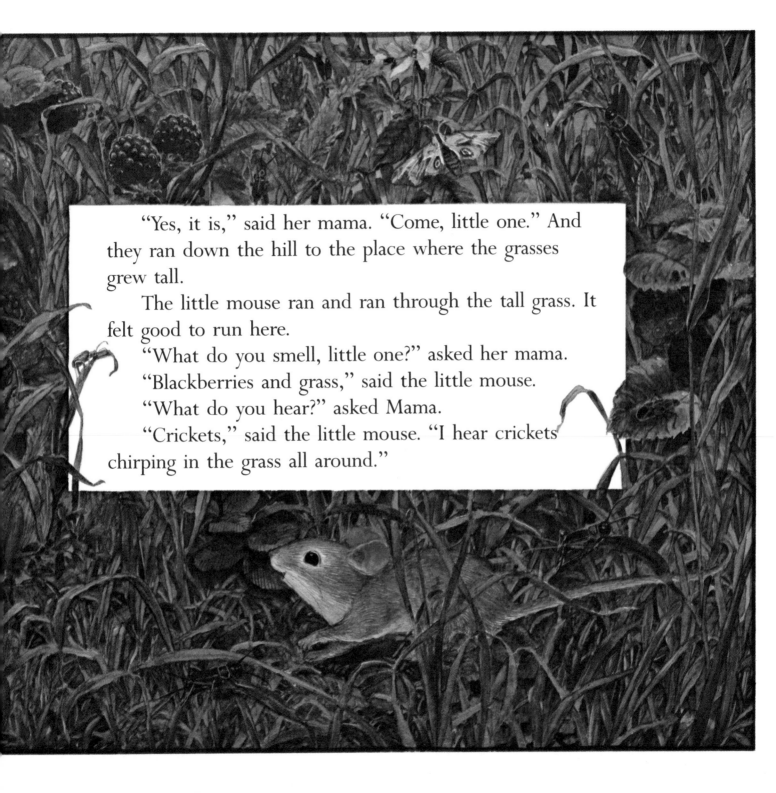

"Yes, it is," said her mama. "Come, little one." And they ran down the hill to the place where the grasses grew tall.

The little mouse ran and ran through the tall grass. It felt good to run here.

"What do you smell, little one?" asked her mama.

"Blackberries and grass," said the little mouse.

"What do you hear?" asked Mama.

"Crickets," said the little mouse. "I hear crickets chirping in the grass all around."

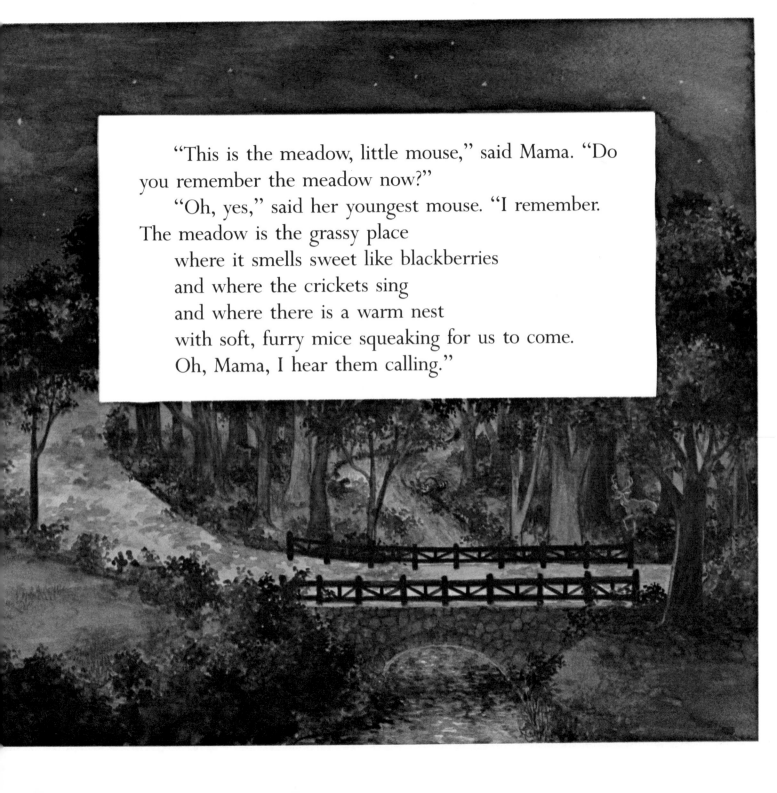

"This is the meadow, little mouse," said Mama. "Do you remember the meadow now?"

"Oh, yes," said her youngest mouse. "I remember. The meadow is the grassy place
where it smells sweet like blackberries
and where the crickets sing
and where there is a warm nest
with soft, furry mice squeaking for us to come.
Oh, Mama, I hear them calling."

"So, little one," asked her mama, "do you know where you live now?"

"I live here!" said the little mouse. "I live here in the meadow...

under the moon."